What Makes Me a Whore?

THE DR. CAGE CHRONICLES:
MEMOIRS OF A SEX THERAPIST

What Makes Me a Whore?

GRAYSON ACE

4 Horsemen
Publications, Inc.

Chapter 1

DANGLING

Getting over Drew proved to be a lot harder that I had anticipated it would be. Even though I was filling my nights with some of the hottest men in the Bay area, after an hour of sucking and fucking, they would go back home, and I would lie in bed, reaching for my phone and looking for the next cock to conquer. Sure, I enjoy sex, but sex does no comparison to the company of someone you love.

After my session the other night with Drew's ex-boyfriend, Anthony, I was starting to feel better about the entire thing. Knowing that Drew did the same shit to another guy, specifically the guy he cheated on me with, was a bit of a comfort for me. It was nice knowing that I wasn't the reason for the break-up, and the Drew really was just a piece of shit. The best part about this was that I was now going to get some private time with Anthony, and I was certainly going to give him and experience he wouldn't forget.

Anthony's appointment was scheduled for the next night, and I needed to figure a way to really make it worth it, not just for me, but for him, too. I started talking to Rocky about the situation and told him I needed some help devising the perfect plan. I think at this point, Rocky had gone through more men in San Francisco than I had, so I knew he had to have some tricks up his sleeve. "Don't worry. I got you."

I swear, after breaking up with Drew, I was horny pretty much every single day. I would randomly pop boners in the most inopportune times, and I found myself constantly swiping through the apps to find another hookup.

I decided to head out to the club that night, hoping to maybe land a little action. I hadn't been to Hard Richards in a while and figured if I couldn't find someone to hook up with, then at least I could pay for some action there. As I was walking out, Jackie asked me if I wanted to grab dinner, but I told her that I had some work to do in the office. No way did I want to hear her lecturing me about going to the club.

I walked inside, and it was pretty busy for a Thursday night. There were two guys up on the stage, one sitting down on a chair while the other guy was doing almost a handstand in front of him, his dick dangling upside down in front of his face. Just the sight of that alone started getting me going. I sat down at the bar to order a drink and began looking around, browsing through the crowd to see if anyone caught my eye.

Fucking Nick. Of course he was there. Why wouldn't he be there? He worked there. We made eye contact for just a second, and I quickly grabbed my drink and got up from the bar before he could come over. Sure, I could fuck him, but he would be the easy fuck. I wanted something new – something a little different. I walked over towards the stage and waited for the show to end. I was imagining that the guy doing the handstand was pretty flexible, and I certainly wouldn't mind seeing what kind of positions he could put me in.

As he walked off the stage towards the back of the club, I grabbed his arm and pulled him off towards the side. I have no clue where my level of courage was coming from, but it's almost as if something else had gotten into me. I leaned in towards his ear and asked if he was available. I'm assuming that what people said when they were trying to go into one of the private rooms.

He laughed a little bit. "I'm flattered, but I'm straight." I saw the way he was dangling that cock in the dude's face. He might claim to be straight, but there's no way he actually was.

"I'll make it worth it." I pulled out a few hundred-dollar bills and held them in my hand in front of him. He looked at the money, looked around for a second, and then started walking away. I started putting the money back in my pocket when I heard him yell to me. "You coming?" He was standing at the door to one of the private rooms, and I quickly walked right in.

He shut the door behind me and told me he only had fifteen minutes until his next performance. He pulled his shorts down sat down on the black leather couch with his arms spread across the back. I didn't waste any time before dropping go my knees right in front of him. He grabbed onto the back of my head and shoved it down towards his balls. His cock was already rock hard, and he pulled it up to expose a set of balls that was hanging right down onto the couch.

I stuck my tongue out underneath his knockers and attempted to suck them both into my mouth. They were a little salty tasting from his sweat and had a texture that made me want to go crazy. I stuck my tongue in and out, rubbing it all over his sack and wrapping my lips around it. I looked up to see his head resting on the back of the couch, his hand still holding onto the back of my head, not wanting to let me go. I moved my tongue up his balls to the base of his cock before creeping my way up to the tip of his head.

His dick was a whole lot bigger once you got up close to it, with a slight curve to the left. I wrapped my mouth around his head, pushing myself down to the base and back up again. He let out a loud moan, and I started bobbing my head up and down faster and faster. At this point I didn't even care if we fucked – I was getting all the action I needed from sucking on his monster. I unzipped my pants and pulled my cock out into my hand, stroking it while going up and down on his tool.

He pulled my head up to his face, and I went in for a kiss. He stopped me just as I was about to lock my lips on his. "Get on your knees."

I didn't hesitate for one minute. I quickly pushed my pants down to my ankles and knelt down on the side of the couch. He got behind me, and I heard him spit on his hand before rubbing his saliva on my hole. He got it nice and wet, and I felt him begin to push his cock against me. He barely got his head in and I was already beginning to scream. I told him he needed some more spit, and I felt him spit down on his dick and my hole, rubbing the moisture all over with his free fingers.

He pushed his cock in some more, and I could feel the pre-cum oozing from my dick. Once it felt like he was completely inside of me, I reached behind me and grabbed onto his hips, holding him in for just a minute so I could stretch out a bit. He grabbed the back of my neck and pushed my face into the back of the couch, and just started going absolutely crazy on my ass. The pain of his semi-dry cock slamming my insides was excruciating and exhilarating at the same time. He held tight onto my hips as he slammed his cock in and out of my hole, and I was grabbing onto the back of the couch just to keep myself positioned.

He pounded away at me for what felt like forever, and yet I think it may have only been two or three minutes. Before I knew it, he let out a loud moan, and gave one final thrust into my hole that felt like a rocket taking off. I could feel his cum shooting deep inside me, oozing out of my hole in between the skin of my ass and his cock. He pulled his dick out and it felt like the floodgates had opened. I could feel a river of his cum flowing out of my hole, and I didn't even care.

I was still on my knees and he grabbed me by the side of my hips and rolled me onto my back.

"Your turn."

He grabbed my cock and shoved it into his mouth, moving his lips up and down my shaft with three of his fingers back in my hole. With the size of his hands, it felt like he was fucking me again. He wasn't even sucking my dick for twenty seconds before I started shooting my load right down his throat. I expected him to spit my cum out on the floor, and to my surprise he swallowed every last drop. He got up from the floor, grabbed his towel and headed for the door.

"See ya soon."

I never did pay him.

Chapter 2

THE REVENGE

I was a little bummed that I never got the guy's name from Richards. I was half-tempted to text Nick and ask him, but that would have just been weird, and also would have opened up an entirely new conversation. I knew I'd probably go back to the bar the next night anyways, and hopefully I could get another taste of his package.

The next morning, I had to wake Rocky up to get into the office in time for Anthony's appointment. One the drive there, Rocky told me his entire plan, and I knew it had to be executed perfectly and the timing had to be spot on in order to work.

We pulled up to the office and Anthony was already there, sitting on the bench in front of the window. He got a huge grin on his face as we were approaching the building, and I could only assume that he had finally heard about my treatment plans from some of his friends. He stood up from the bench, and it was evident that he wasn't wearing any underwear, because I could see a perfect outline of his dick through his gym shorts, and there's no way he didn't catch me staring.

His monster looked huge.

He may have been a total bottom, but we were about to change all that. I greeted him while Rocky opened up the office and told him to take a seat while we got things prepared. I had a few notes to enter into the system and told Rocky to show Anthony to the therapy room. I was actually feeling a bit nervous, because this wasn't just another therapy session to me. This was like the closing of a chapter. I couldn't help but get a little sad thinking about what was about to happen, but the sadness quickly faded as the blood started rushing to my dick because of the thoughts of what was about to occur.

I walked back towards the therapy room and was actually taken back by what I saw when I opened the door.

Anthony. Butt ass naked on the couch. Ass up. Head down.

"I knew what I wanted as soon as I met you at my last appointment, and I'm gonna get it." He never even turned around to make sure it was me and not Rocky walking in on him. Although, he definitely wouldn't have complained either way. I shut the door behind me and pulled off my shirt as I approached the couch. I started unzipping my pants, but I didn't even want to waste any time. He had such a hot little ass, and his hole looked nearly perfect.

I dropped down behind him, pants barely pulled down past my hips, and grabbed onto his ass cheeks to spread them and get a better look. I stuck out my tongue and barely pressed it against the bottom of his hole and his back arched like a surprised cat. I circled my tongue around his hole, slowly, before diving straight in. His ass tasted amazing, and he was letting out some pretty loud moans.

I made my way down to his balls, rubbing his hole with my thumb and sliding it in and out. I grabbed onto his dick and pulled it down so I could get a little taste, licking the tip before wrapping my lips around the head of it. I could tell he wanted to sink down into the couch in ecstasy, and at one point I had to kind of push him back up onto his knees.

I grabbed onto his hips and flipped him over onto his back so I could get a better angle of his dick. He obviously wasn't shy and wanted the same thing that I did, because he grabbed my head and shoved my face right back down onto his throbbing cock.

It tasted delicious.

I wrapped my hand around the base and moved my mouth up and down, twirling my tongue around his head with every bob. He was a real squirmer, and I thought at one point he was going to slide right off the couch. I shoved a few fingers into his hole while slobbing on his dick, and he grabbed my hand to control the motion, faster and faster.

I stood up and pulled him towards the edge of the couch. He grabbed onto my pants and finished pulling them down around my ankles. I was rock hard and already pre-cumming. He licked the cum from the tip of my dick and devoured the entire thing. I could feel my cock going right into his throat, and this guy didn't even flinch at all – no gag reflex.

I grabbed onto the back of his head and pulled him into my groin, trying to get something out of him, because it was almost making me a little insecure. He was a pro.

Anthony started stroking my cock as he was sucking it, and it was like a vortex on my tool. It felt so amazing, and I really wanted to feel his insides. I pushed him onto his back, and he grabbed onto his legs and pulled them towards the back of the couch. He wanted it just as badly as I did. I reached for the lube and was about to open the bottle when he swatted it out of my hands. "No lube, just spit." I was totally down. I spit down in my hands and rubbed it over the head of my cock and put a little bit into his hole. I was still holding his legs back as I pressed the head of my penis against his hole. I thought for sure that I would need lube, but that thing just slid right in.

For a total bottom, he felt really tight. His moist hole swallowed my cock, and it felt really amazing. Drew obviously didn't know what he was missing out on. I pushed my dick all the way in until it couldn't go any further, and then pulled it the entire way out so I could watch his hole move. I put it back in slowly, and then just started pounding away. I leaned down into Anthony so we could make out, and he was holding onto his feet straight into the air, giving me total access to his hole.

I turned around to look at the clock, and knew I had to make this last a few more minutes. I pulled my dick out to give myself a break and leaned down to eat his ass some more. It was nice and loose, and my tongue was sliding right inside of it. He grabbed onto my hair and pulled my face in, not wanting me to leave for even a second.

I kissed my way up his chest and made out some more, and then I heard the entrance bell ring, just barely. I spit on my dick and got it nice and wet again and shoved my cock right back into his hole as hard as I could. He was still holding onto his feet, and I grabbed his hips and started fucking him like a jack hammer. He was letting out some loud screams, and then I heard the door open behind me.

"What the fuck?"

As soon as I heard those words, I turned around, and there was Drew. His jaw was on the floor, and I didn't even care.

"I'm gonna cum." That was all I needed. Seeing him and his face was all I needed. I let out a huge sigh of relief and shot my load right up Anthony's wet hole. I kept fucking him so I could get every last drop and turned around and smiled at Drew as I continued thrusting my dick in and out. He didn't even know what to say. Anthony leaned over once he finally realized someone had opened the door.

"What the fuck, Drew. What are you doing here?" Anthony grabbed his shirt to cover up his pre-cumming dick. "Don't worry," I said. "He just forgot something."

Rocky grabbed Drew by the arm and led him back towards the reception area. I could Rocky talking to him. "I'm so sorry you had to see that. I guess I was wrong – your keys were over here the entire time."

This was the revenge I had wanted, and it was all Rocky's idea. He had purposely set this entire thing up so that Drew would walk in on us, and I finally had the closure that I deserved, but also had a hot fucking guy that I needed something else from.

I was still rock hard and still inside of Anthony's ass, and I could tell he was super confused by what had just happened.

"Why did my ex-boyfriend just walk in?" I told him that Drew and I had dated, and that he had done the same thing to me that he had done to him, and that I just wanted some revenge. Anthony got a little grin on his face.

"Well then, since you used me, now I get to use you."

He threw his shirt behind the couch and grabbed my shoulders, lifting me up from in front of him and pulling me towards him. I strattled his dick and started kissing him, rubbing my ass over his cock. I knew what he wanted, and I'm pretty sure he knew that I wanted it. While we were making out, I grabbed the lube and poured it into my hands, rubbing it all over his cock and on my hole. I grabbed onto his tool and moved it until I could feel it pressing against my hole and lowered myself onto it.

It's always a shame when guys with such nice dicks don't want to top. It's like they have no clue how much they are depriving the world of what they have to offer. Even though I already came I was still rock hard, and as I was riding his dick, he was stroking mine. I bounced up and down, leaning in to kiss him and wanted him to fuck me all night. I could tell I was getting close to cumming again and told him I wanted his load. He got the same grin on his face that he had before and started fucking me harder and faster. He let out a loud moan, and as soon as I felt him do one final thrust into my hole, I started shooting my load all over his chest. I could feel his load flooding my hole, and knew he was either a heavy cummer or just had been saving it. When I got up off of his cock, his jizz dripped out of my like a firehose.

We both put our clothes back on, and as he walked out the door, he mentioned that we didn't even get to talk about anything during the session. I told him to make an appointment on his way out and we could see what we could accomplish.

"Oh, I think we already accomplished a lot."

And that was how I finally got over my ex.

Chapter 3

LUCAS

All this recent bottoming really had me hornier than ever, and all I could think about after my recent revenge conquer was where I could get some more dick from. I walked out into reception to talk to Rocky, but he was already gone. Knowing him, he was probably in the back alley fucking Drew. I doubt it, but even if it was true, I wouldn't even be mad. I locked up the office and started browsing through the apps to see if I could get some action on the way home.

As I was scrolling through profiles, I stumbled across one of my friends, Lucas, and figured why not see what he was up to. I shot him a text message, and I was barely even able to his send when he was already responding. I didn't even want to make small talk, so I got straight to the point. "Hey, I'm horny. Wanna fuck?" Of course, his response was a yes, so I got into my car and headed over to his house.

It had been quite some time since the last time I had hooked up with Lucas. He was primarily a bottom, but I was really in the mood for his dick and was hoping he'd be down for it. I got to his house and knocked on the door, and as soon as he opened it up, he gave me a huge hug. Lucas was such a sweet guy, and if he weren't such a whore, I probably would have wanted to date him.

We made small talk for a couple of minutes and then I told him we should head up to his bedroom. We walked upstairs and I noticed he had a candle lit and the lube on his nightstand. I'm surprised he didn't have a condom waiting as well, but it was a raw dog kind of day and I was willing to be a little risky with him.

This wasn't going to be the normal undress each other while we kiss kind of hook-up. We both knew I had come over to fuck, so I took off all my clothes before hopping into bed and under the covers, and Lucas followed behind me. He got under the covers with me, and I pulled him over, feeling his body against mine and we started making out. I always loved the feeling of another naked body against mine, rubbing our cocks together and moving our hands all over each other. He kept grabbing onto my ass and playing with my hole while we were kissing, which was kind of surprising because I thought he was going to try and bottom.

I pushed him over on his back and started kissing his neck, moving my way down to his chest and stomach before feeling the tip of his dick against my chin. I grabbed onto his balls and pulled them down to make his dick pop up and started sucking on it. He grabbed onto my head and held onto it as I went up and down, thrusting his hips up into the air.

I got up after a few minutes and made my way up towards his face, on my knees with my dick right at his mouth. I grabbed onto the back of his head and pulled it towards me, him willingly opening his mouth and taking my entire dick. I started fucking his face and he reached around, and I could feel his finger rubbing on my hole with his other hand stroking his dick. I knew he enjoyed getting face fucked, and quite honestly, I loved doing it.

I was still thrusting my dick in and out of his mouth and I told him I wanted him to fuck me. He pushed me away and moved me over so that I was down on my stomach. He got behind me and spread my ass cheeks, and then I felt his tongue fly right into my hole. I didn't think he was a huge fan of eating ass, but maybe his preferences had really changed since the last time we were together.

He laid his body on top of mine, rubbing his cock in between my ass cheeks and kissing my back. At one point he grabbed onto my neck and bit my ear a little bit, and that alone almost made be blow. I'm not sure what had gotten into him or where Lucas had gone, but I like it.

He leaned over and grabbed the lube and started getting his dick nice and wet. He asked me if I wanted to use a condom, but I said I wanted to feel all of him. He spit on my hole, and then got back on top of me, guiding his dick right into my hole. I was obviously still pretty loose, so it took no effort at all to get inside of me. He laid flat against my body with his arms wrapped under me around my chest and started thrusting his hips up and down, his dick going in and out, and it felt really good.

He kept kissing on my neck and pulling it a little bit as we were fucking, and I just kept thinking what a shame it was that we couldn't date, because I could have totally seen myself liking this guy. But a fuck is all it was going to be.

He told me to push my ass back, and I knew he wanted to hit it doggy style, so I pushed myself up so that his dick wouldn't fall out of my ass. He grabbed onto my hips and started slamming his cock deep inside of me, and I could feel his big balls bouncing against mine. I started jerking my cock because I knew I wasn't going to last very long. He kept pounding away at my ass and asked if he could cum inside, and before I could even say yes, I felt his load filling my hole. We both started laughing, and he pulled his dick out as soon as he was done and started licking his cum from around my hole.

I kept stroking on my dick, and it's like he knew I was going to cum because he rolled over on his back and put his face underneath my cock and started sucking on it. I shot my load down his through and he started gagging a little bit. He moved his head to give himself a chance to swallow my cum, and then started sucking on it again, getting every last drop. I turned my body around and started making out with him again for a few minutes.

My phone started going off and it was a message from Mike, this married guy I had met online. I was exhausted, but certainly wasn't going to miss out on this opportunity. I jumped out of bed, threw on my clothes and ran towards the door.

"When can I see you again?" I wasn't sure if I wanted to see Lucas again or not, but knew he'd be a back-up next time I was horny.

"Soon."

We never spoke again.

Chapter 4

BYRON

I drove home from Lucas's house and was already popping a boner thinking about Mike. Mike was this married guy I met on one of the apps, and we had been messaging back and forth for a few weeks. I hadn't been with many married guys, and never missed out on the opportunity. There was something so different about getting into bed with a straight, married man – you could never predict what the experience would be like.

Some straight men are super masculine in bed. A lot of times they are either strict tops, or they are total bottoms letting out their inner fantasies, but they are almost never a mix of the two. Sometimes it's just a guy trying to get his dick sucked because his wife won't, or his wife doesn't put out that often anymore. Other times, it's just a guy stuck in a fake life, pretending to be straight but is actually deep down in love with me, but for whatever reason could never be his true self. Either way, I don't care – give me some manly dick.

It took a while to get something set up with Mike. He needed to be a little sneaky because of his wife, and he said the best time to come over would be the middle of the night. I was a little surprised by this, because most men wouldn't try to sneak out of the house with their wives in bed next to them. He said that his wife took sleeping medicine every night and slept like a horse and wasn't at all concerned.

When I finally got home from the office, I sat in the driveway for a little bit texting with Mike. There was another car in the driveway, and I knew Rocky must have rushed home for some trick. Mike and I were going back and forth a bit, and finally decided to hook up the next night. He said his wife normally went to bed right before midnight, and he'd be over shortly after he knew she was asleep. I wasn't entirely thrilled about the middle-of-the-night session, but a married guy is always worth it.

When I walked into the house, I noticed a pair of pants lying on the couch, and they weren't Rocky's, so I knew he was definitely getting frisky with someone. I was curious who it was, so I checked in the pocket and pulled out the guy's wallet. I looked for his license, and the guy's name was Byron – a 30-year-old good looking black man. I didn't take Rocky for someone who would be attracted to anyone other than guys who look like him, but then again, to Rocky, a hole was a hole.

I walked back towards my bedroom and couldn't help but hear the noise coming from his bedroom. The sound of moaning was a little feminine, and I knew it had to be Byron. Rocky, naturally, never completely shut the door, and I actually think he enjoyed when I would "catch" him in the act. Of course, just like every other time, I wasn't opposed to taking a peek and seeing what was going on.

I peeked through the door and saw Byron on top of Rocky. Rocky was lying on his back with Byron's ass in his face while Byron was sucking on his dick. Byron had pretty long hair, pulled back in a ponytail to keep it out of the way. Brother or not, it was always hot seeing Rocky in action, and I loved watching Byron slob up and down his pole. I was hard almost immediately and unzipped my pants so I could start rubbing my cock.

Byron kept coming up from air and letting out some wild moans, and I could only imagine how deep into his hole Rocky was going. He kept going up and down on his dick, swallowing the entire thing and then slowly coming back up. I pulled my dick out and started stroking it, and I was so focused on what Rocky was doing to his hole that I didn't even realize Byron was watching me. Rocky's cock was still in his mouth, and I could tell by the look in his eyes that he wants to compare brother to brother.

I opened the door and walked in, and I knew that Rocky knew I was there, but that didn't stop him from continuing to bury his face in Byron's ass. I pulled my pants down to my ankles and walked to the edge of the bed. Byron pulled his way over to the edge and opened up his mouth and waited for me to enter. I looked back at Rocky who leaned over towards the side of the bed to grab a condom and some lube out of his nightstand.

I took my dick in my hand and smacked it on the side of Byron's face. He opened his mouth and stuck out his tongue, waiting for me to smack it with my tool, which of course I did. I grabbed him by the back of his head as I shoved my dick right into his throat and waited for him to start moving his head. I saw Rocky slide a condom over his massive dick and lube it up, and he slide up onto Byron who was lying on his stomach, still swallowing my piece.

Rocky guided his dick into Byron's hole, and I could tell when he entered because I felt Byron's mouth get tighter on my dick. Byron kept moving his head forward and backwards, making my dick super wet and wrapping his lips around it as tightly as he could. Rocky was barely rocking his hips, letting his cock penetrate his hole slowly, but still making Byron moan. He was kissing Byron's neck, and this was probably the closest that he had ever had his mouth to my cock. Surprisingly, it didn't weird me out, because we had done this a few times, and at this point it was almost the brotherly equivalent of "no-homo." No-bromo, I guess.

Rocky grabbed onto Byron's ass and pulled it up a little bit and stuffed a pillow underneath his pelvis to keep it a bit heightened. He started pounding his hole harder and harder, and with every thrust it almost felt like my cock was going deeper and deeper into his mouth. I thought the motion of Rocky going to town on his ass would have made him lose concentration on my dick, but it didn't. He kept sucking away, letting out loud moans and almost not even being sidetracked by what my brother was doing to his ass.

Rocky pulled his dick out and sat down on the bed with his head on the pillows. He told Byron to get on top and start riding him. Byron let my dick out of his mouth and turned around and jumped right on top of my brother's cock, not even hesitating as he sat down on it. Rocky grabbed onto his hips and he started thrusting his hips forward and backwards. He turned around and looked at me and sort of nodded for me to come over, so I kicked my pants the rest of the way off and jumped up on the bed.

I stood with my ass resting on the headboard, one leg on each side of Rocky's head. I looked down and saw Rocky looking up at what was hanging over his face – my rock-hard cock and sagging balls. Byron leaned forward and took my cock back into his mouth and started sucking on it really hard. At one point during this, I realized I had lost count of how many times I had cum in the paste 24 hours and wasn't sure if I'd be able to do it again, but I definitely wasn't giving up.

Byron grabbed onto my dick and started stroking it as he was sucking on it, and I knew that was going to be it. I grabbed onto the back of his head and held my dick inside of it as I started filling his mouth with my load. How I still had this much to give, I never figured out. I thought Byron would have swallowed, but he quickly took my cock out of his mouth and kept stroking it while he opened his mouth and let my nut fall down on my brother's chest. He kept stroking me, letting my cum cover the rest of his face.

As soon as I started shooting my load on his face, I head Rocky let out a moan of relief, and knew that he had cum. I was still standing over my brother's head, and Byron got up from my brother's cock and went down to his dick and pulled the condom off, sucking on his dick to get all the cum off. Super confusing – did he like cum or not?

I jumped off the bed and grabbed my pants, letting them finish whatever they still had left to do. I went out into the living room to grab my laptop and get some work done, and saw Byron walking out of Rocky's room as I was heading back towards my room. He smiled and said "see ya soon," and then left.

When I walked into my bedroom, I heard my phone go off, and it was a notification from one of the dating apps. It was Byron, with a picture of his cock, and a message that read "I want you to ride it." And I had every intention of doing just that.

Chapter 5

BACKLASH

I seemed to have been on a bit of a roll, but actually was starting to feel like I needed a break from all the action. Mike, the married guy, was going to be coming over tomorrow night, and I really just needed some time to relax and let my load regain some strength. I decided to commit to no apps for the next 24 hours, so Facebook and Instagram would be my go-to's to fill my time.

I laid in bed and scrolled through Instagram for what must have been a few hours. I had realized that I was spending all of my time looking for hook-ups that I really had no clue what was going on in the non-sexual world with my friends. I was scrolling through and saw a photo that really pissed me off, and was on someone's account who I thought I had deleted and blocked – Hope, Drew's lesbian friend.

It was a picture of Drew, Hope, Dina and Katlyn, all out together at some club, looking like their typical skanky, nasty selves. I read the caption, and immediately knew it was aimed towards me.

"It's the cheaters who always lose in the end."

Now, I didn't know who the fuck they were talking about, although I actually did. This fucker obviously told his friends that it was *me* who had cheated, and completely spun the story around, when it was him who cheated, not just on me, but on Anthony, too. I guarantee he told them that Anthony and I were sleeping together, which is true, but it obviously hadn't happened during either of our relationships.

I sent the post to Rocky and Harry, and I knew they were going to be just as pissed as I was. We all knew the truth – Drew cheated on me and was trying to hide the fact that he was a sleeze ball by telling everyone that it was me who was unfaithful. Rocky, of course, having no qualms, immediately send the post to Drew asking for an explanation, and Drew, of course, replied by stating "everyone knows it was Hunter who cheated."

I was beyond livid at this point. I wanted so bad to message all three of his little bitchy friends, but knew they were going to just side with him. Of course, they would, I'd expect my friends to side with me as well. It just really sucked, because I thought they were my friends, too. They obviously don't know who the real Drew is, because cheating was simply a part of his DNA.

Prior to this, I never really cared what people thought about me. I know my truth, but seeing stuff like this on social media, where we have plenty of other mutual friends really just pissed me off. Here was Drew, telling his sob story about how everyone did him wrong, when it was actually him who did everyone else wrong. I wanted to get back, but I really wasn't sure how to. And then, out of nowhere, I remembered the story that Anthony had told me about his experience with Drew and Hope, and I decided that was the angle I could take.

I went back to the post on Instagram and must have written and deleted my comment a dozen times before getting it just right to ensure it made the right impact.

"@drew @dina @hope @katlyn: it may be the cheaters who always lose in the end, but at least I don't need one of these to prove a point." And underneath my comment, I inserted a photoshopped picture of Hope and Drew, mostly naked with a dildo in Hope's hand, just like the one she used on Anthony.

Chapter 6

MIKE

The whole Instagram things really had me lit, and my comment alone wasn't enough for me to get back at them. As always, I talked about it with Rocky, asking for his help to create the perfect plan to get some revenge. I'm not sure who I wanted revenge on more – Drew, or his three cunty friends. Either way, I knew I could count on Rocky to really come up with the perfect plan. In reality, I'd love to shove a dildo up my ass, shit on it, and then send one to all of them, but that would just be a waste. I needed more. And even though I was really pissed, and a little hurt, by the way his friends were acting, I knew Drew was a driving force behind what was going on, and he was the one I needed revenge on. Just having him catch me and Anthony fucking wasn't enough.

I woke up pretty excited the next day, knowing that Mike was coming over. Hookups normally didn't get my excited, but anytime it was with a straight, married man, I always got a little giddy thinking about it. He wasn't coming over until way later that night though, and I kind of felt like a kid on Christmas Eve waiting for Santa to come, not knowing what gifts he'd be bringing.

I spent the day just relaxing and hanging out at the pool. There were a couple of really hot college guys at the pool, and it was so hard resisting the temptation of just walking up to them and asking if I could suck their dicks. It's funny – when I lived in Pennsylvania, I never would have thought about just approaching a guy and offering some type of sexual service. I was always terrified that if I ever approached someone like that, that I would get my ass kicked. In San Fran, it really didn't matter, and that was almost a part of the gay culture. There were two of them, and every time they got out of the pool, I could see a perfect outline of their cocks through their swim trunks, and I really wanted to just walk over to them, drop to my knees and swallow their monsters. But I needed to be good, because let's be honest. Me sucking their dicks would turn into someone's dick going into someone's ass, and I really wanted to save my load for Mike.

Later that night I decided it was time to get ready before I laid down for a little nap. I needed to save up my energy – I knew it was going to be a long night, and I actually had a new patient coming at 9 in the morning the next day.

I did the standard "getting ready" procedures for when I knew I'd be bottoming. Of course, I really wanted to top Mike, but as a straight married man, I assumed he'd be the one sticking it in me. It would be an added bonus if he let me near his hole, but I wouldn't be holding my breath, and wanted to make sure I was extra prepared for him.

I fell asleep on the couch but set an alarm for around midnight since I knew that's when he'd be messaging me. I woke up to the sound of my alarm and was shocked to see that I had received a message from Mike about five minutes earlier. "I'm here." I'm assuming he didn't knock on the door, and I started panicking thinking he might have left since I didn't respond. I ran to the door, and he wasn't there, so then I started getting really nervous. I was fucking tonight no matter what. I grabbed my phone and called him. He had just gotten back into his car and was going to leave because he thought I had flaked out. I did one of my nervous laughs, and then said something super corny, but told him to get back to my door.

I opened the door as he was approaching. He looked a little different in person than he did on the apps, but not in a bad way. He was a little darker complected, possibly Middle Eastern, and had a bald head, which was actually a total turn-on for me. He was always wearing ball caps in any of the pictures he sent me. He worked out a lot, and had really nice arms and a small, sexy waist, and barely had some chin stubble. All in all, he was pretty hot. As he approached the door, he held out his hand to shake mine, which was a typical straight guy thing to say. I shook his hand and let him in, closing the door behind him and actually feeling a little nervous about what was going to happen.

I led him back to my bedroom and closed the door behind me. I knew if I had left the door open that Rocky probably would have started watching, and I really wasn't in the mood to share. I turned around and Mike grabbed my arms and pulled me over to him. He shoved his tongue right down my throat and started making out with me, pulling my hips towards his so our cocks would rub together. He was wearing jogging pants, and it was obvious that he didn't have any underwear on, and I of course didn't put any on under my gym shorts.

He was rubbing his hands all over me while we made out, and I grabbed his hat off the top of his head and threw it across the room. We were still standing in front of my bed, pulling off each other's shirts, exposing his extremely chiseled chest. I started kissing his neck, and then went down and started sucking on his nipple. I felt his body tremor, and he started making some noises, and I knew he had some sensitive nipples and that I was going to have to give them plenty of attention.

I sucked on one nipple for a minute while squeezing the other, and then swapped sided, before kissing my way down to his waist. I held onto his hips and he placed his hands on my head, guiding me down to his special area. I started licking the outside of his pants, finding his cock with my mouth and wrapping my lips around it. He wasn't hard yet but had a dick that seemed to hang pretty low, and I loved rubbing my mouth on it over his pants. I grabbed the waistband and pulled his pants down, licking from the base of his cock down to the head before opening my lips and letting the entire thing inside. I took his entire dick back down to the base and wrapped my lips as tightly as I could, making that monster grow inside of my mouth. With my lips shut and tongue moving all over the place, I could feel it growing inside of my mouth, and within seconds I had to back up, so I didn't choke on it.

I grabbed onto his dick and started stroking it inside of my mouth. He must have just had a really sensitive body – about every five seconds he would let out a little shiver, like every inch of him was "the spot." He turned and leaned against the edge of the bed to give himself some support, and I just kept on sucking and sucking – his cock tasted so good.

He pulled me back up and started kissing me again. I kicked my shorts off while we were kissing and turned to get on the bed. I wanted to feel him on top of me, and he was such a good kisser that I wasn't ready for anything else to happen. I laid down with my head on the pillows, and he crawled back up towards me, giving my dick just a little lick as he passed by it. He laid his body flat against mine and started rubbing his cock against mine as he kissed me all over my chest, neck and lips.

After a few minutes he went down and swallowed my tool, taking every single inch of it. His mouth felt wet and warm, and the tightness almost made it feel like an ass when I would close my eyes. He didn't have any hair to grab, so I held onto the back of his head, gently pressing it down and holding it as he came back up. He licked one of his fingers and slowly inserted it into my hole as he continued to suck, and I thought that he was going to make me cum. I grabbed him by the shoulders and pulled him back up towards my face to continue kissing.

"You're going to make me cum."

We both laughed and started kissing again. The way he was sucking my dick and kissing me – there's no way this guy was 100% straight. He had told me that I wasn't the only guy he messed around with and said that there were a few others. In reality, I'm thinking this guy had probably been with as many guys as I had been with. But I had to keep him away from my dick, because I knew that every time he went down there he'd be getting me close to an explosion.

Mike kept going back and forth from my dick to my mouth, sucking me off until I'd pull him back up to prevent me from blowing. I could tell this guy really liked being with another man, and I wasn't upset about it. After about an hour and a half of this back and forth, I really wanted him to fuck me. As soon as I said that he reached over and grabbed a condom and put it on, and I rubbed some lube on his dick. He lifted my legs into the air and pressed his cock against my hole, and for some odd reason I was really tight. He kept pressing his dick against me, and it just wouldn't go in. I'm not sure if he was nervous, or if I was just extra tight for some reason. Well, obviously I was.

I pulled the condom off and turned around so I could start sucking on him again. He had lost some of his boner and was a little limp, so I figured he might just need some help. As soon as I put his dick in my mouth, I could feel it get erect again. I sucked on it for a few minutes while he rubbed his fingers on my hole, and then told him we needed to try again.

I rolled back over on my back and pulled him towards me to start kissing again. I could feel him rubbing his dick on my hole, and grabbed it to start guiding it in. He pulled back and said that he needed to wear a condom. I told him it would go in a bit more easily if we just went without a condom and promised that I was clean. I could tell he was hesitant, and probably heard that from all the guys he fucked around with or picked up something nasty from one of them. I hated using condoms and just really wanted to feel him inside of me, raw. He reached over and grabbed another condom, and I started joking around that he would love my ass way more if he could feel it without the added layer.

He put the condom on anyways and lubed up again, and we went through the same process. I was still super tight, and he was losing his boner again, and I flipped around and went back down and started sucking his dick again. He did the same shiver and moan and was immediately rock hard again. I turned around and got back on my back, and he got on top of me and started rubbing his cock on my hole again. I grabbed it, and this time got the head of his penis inside my hole. He got a huge smile on his face and must not have realized that he wasn't wearing a condom. He held it there for a minute, and then looked down and realized he was inside of me raw. He pulled out and said we needed to use a condom, which I knew at this point just wasn't going to work for us.

I pushed him over on his back and started sucking on his dick again, stroking it really tightly with my hands while it went in and out of my mouth. I kept jerking on it and told him I wanted him to blow his load in my mouth. At this point, it was 3am, and I was exhausted and needed to get some sleep before I had to be to work. I kept sucking on his dick for the next ten minutes and he wasn't even getting close, so I licked one of my fingers and barely stuck it inside his hole. He was either going to smack me or blow his load immediately, and luckily it was the latter. No sooner did my finger enter him was he filling my mouth with his batter, and I swallowed every last drop.

I got up and knelt over his chest, pulling his head up so he could suck on me. He had his hands behind his head, propping it up for a better angle, and just as he knew I was about to cum he pulled my cock out of his mouth and started jerking me off. He obviously wasn't into swallowing, which was fine by me, because he still let me shoot my load all over his face.

I grabbed him a towel to wipe off and asked if he wanted to shower. I assumed he wouldn't want to go home with the scent of man sex all over him. He declined, and I asked if he wanted to do it again.

"Fuck ya. I'm going to get inside of you no matter what it takes."

And I was determined to get him inside of me, no matter what it would take.

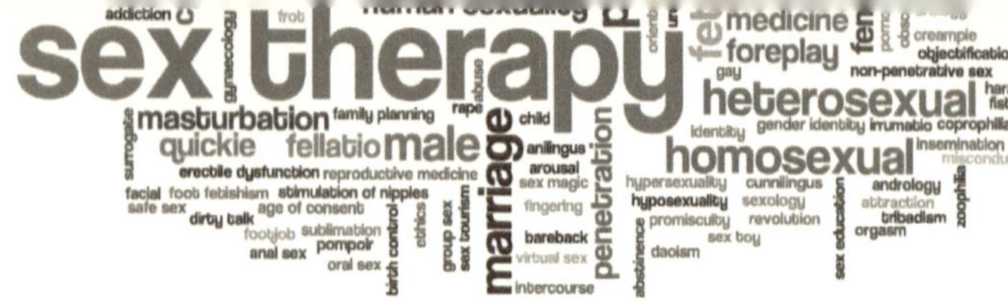

Chapter 7

REVENGE, SQUARED

I knew that there was no way I'd be in any condition to see a new patient just a few hours after such a marathon, so I sent out and email clearing my following day and rescheduled the new patient for the following week. I was just about to fall asleep when I heard Rocky go into his bedroom, and I decided to see if he had figured anything out for our revenge plan.

I walked into his bedroom and he started explaining his ideas to me, which were pure genius. I'm not sure why, but he always seemed to come up with the perfect ideas. He asked me some pretty specific questions about Drew, and then said that he'd handle everything and let me know what I needed to do next. The thought of his plan got me excited, but also made me think if this is really the person I was. But that thought faded pretty quickly, and the thought of how this would all go down really made everything worth it.

The next morning, Rocky sent me a message with a time and an address, and a few small directions of how to navigate the building. I didn't recognize the address but google showed that it was some old warehouse. I asked him what I was supposed to do when I got there, and he said it would just come naturally.

I pulled up to the address and followed his directions through the building until I came to a closed door. There was a sign on the door that said to enter quietly. I opened the door, and the room was barely lit, but I could see a figure on the mattress at the other end of the room. As I approached, I could better make out what was on the mattress – a naked man, head down in a pillow, blind-folded, and raw ass up in the air. There was a sign hanging on the wall next to the mattress. "Breed me."

I knew Rocky was into some weird shit, but I wasn't sure what this had to do with getting revenge, but I also wasn't going to pass up on a sweet ass. I pulled my pants down and started stroking my cock while I rubbed my thumb on the sweet hole in front of me. I knelt down on the edge of the mattress to get closer to this fine ass and dove my face right inside. They guy started moaning, and I could tell that he wasn't just blind-folded, but he was also gagged. This was some really kinky bondage shit, and I was kind of into it.

I shoved my tongue deep inside this hole and reached around and started stroking the dude's dick, and the ass tasted oddly familiar. I didn't think an ass would ever remind you of someone, but it oddly tasted like something I had before, but with my body count, there'd be no way to really know who it was.

I kept stroking my dick until I was rock hard and grabbed the lube off the floor next to the mattress to get myself nice and wet. I pulled the guy closer to the edge of the mattress so I could kneel down and get inside of him. I slapped my cock on his hole which made his back bend down a little bit. I pressed the head against him, slowly putting in every inch I had. Normally I'd give someone a little time to adjust to me, but something got ahold of me and made me just go to town. I grabbed that guy's hips and started fucking him as fast and as hard as I could. I'm not sure if I knew who he was or not, or if I knew what he liked, but I knew I wanted to make him hurt just a little bit

I could hear him screaming through the gag, muffling out the words "harder, harder." I kept on pounding him as hard as I could and ripped my sweaty shirt off. There was sweat dripping from my head all over him and down my chest. I pushed him down flat on the mattress and wrapped my arms around his neck to help myself get a better grip and thrusted my hips into him as hard as I could.

There was something about this anonymous hookup that really got me going. I'd normally want to flip the guy over and make out and suck his dick and choke him with mine but thrusting myself into him not knowing who he was really had me turned on, and it didn't take long until my dick started exploding and filling this guy's hole with my load. I kept fucking as hard as I could, feeling the cum shoot out between thrusts. I gave one final push inside of him to drain my monster out, and then just laid on top of him for a minute trying to catch my breath.

I got off of him and started putting my clothes back on before leaving the room. I grabbed my phone and saw that I had a message from Rocky asking how it was.

"Probably the hottest time of my life. Thanks for setting this up. But when's the revenge plan going to be put into action?"

He responded. "Wasn't that revenge enough?"

I was just about to leave the room when I saw that message. No. This couldn't have been. Really?

I walked back over and turned the light so that I could see who I had just manhandled. He was still lying there, obviously trying to catch his breath, and I noticed a very familiar birthmark on the side of his hip.

It was Drew.

And that was all the revenge that I needed.

Author Bio

Grayson Ace has had his fair share of sexcapades, and figured why not write about them? Recently divorced, he is re-discovering himself (and plenty of hot men) and creating many new sexy adventures along the way. If you like what you see, please leave a review, and you never know....you may end up in one of the stories!

GraysonAce.com
Facebook: Grayson Ace
Instagram: graysonaceofficial
Twitter: @GraysonAce1

More Books From

Grayson Ace

How I Got Here
First Year Out of the Closet
You're Only a Top?
You're Only a Bottom?
I Think I'm a Serial Swiper
Lookin' in All the Wrong Places
What Makes Me a Whore?
A Breach in Confidentiality
Back Door Pass
My European Adventure
An Unexpected Affair
More to come!

4 Horsemen Publications

LGBT Erotica

Leo Sparx
Before Alexander
Claiming Alexander
Taming Alexander
Saving Alexander

Erotica

Ali Whippe
Office Hours
Tutoring Center
Athletics
Extra Credit
Bound for Release
Fetish Circuit

Dalia Lance
My Home on Whore Island
Slumming It on Slut Street
Training of the Tramp
The Imperfect Perfection
72% Match
It Was Meant To Be... Or Whatever

CHASTITY VELDT

Molly in Milwaukee
Irene in Indianapolis
Lydia in Louisville
Natasha in Nashville
Alyssa in Atlanta

HONEY CUMMINGS

Sleeping with Sasquatch
Cuddling with Chupacabra
Naked with New Jersey Devil
Laying with the Lady in Blue
Wanton Woman in White
Beating it with Bloody Mary
Beau and Professor Bestialora
The Goat's Gruff
Goldie and Her Three Beards
Pied Piper's Pipe
Princess Pea's Bed
Jack's Beanstalk

4HorsemenPublications.com